BIG BEAR
LITTLE BROTHER

To Dominique Demers, from her bear – C.N.

To the last remaining polar bears – K.O.

First published 2009 by Macmillan Children's Books
This edition published 2011 by Macmillan Children's Books
a division of Macmillan Publishers Limited
20 New Wharf Road, London N1 9RR
Basingstoke and Oxford
Associated companies throughout the world
www.panmacmillan.com

ISBN: 978-1-4472-0274-5

Text copyright © Carl Norac 2009
Illustrations copyright © Kristin Oftedal 2009
Moral rights asserted

3 5 7 9 8 6 4

A CIP catalogue record for this book is available from the British Library.

Printed in China

Carl Norac

BIG BEAR
LITTLE BROTHER

Illustrated by Kristin Oftedal

Macmillan Children's Books

On the ice, with the wind blowing gently, Big Bear stopped running. How wonderful it was to be still . . . to close his eyes . . . to dream!

Suddenly he heard a cry from the cliff above. Who was it? Was it a hunter? He looked up quickly.

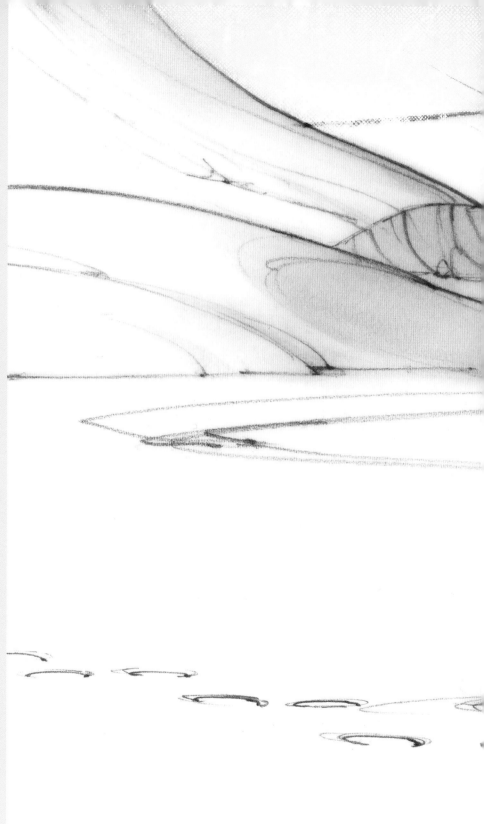

A child was tumbling through the sky, just like a snowflake.
He must have slipped and fallen. He'd be crushed on the hard ice!
Big Bear ran, dived . . .

. . . and caught him safely
in his huge paws.

The little boy trembled when he realised where he had landed.
"Don't be scared," said Big Bear.
He put the boy down and started on his way.

But soon he heard a voice behind him.
"Wait! I'm Minik! I'm coming with you."

They walked side by side until they
reached an ice bridge. Then Big Bear
went ahead, slowly . . . carefully . . .
to make sure the ice was thick enough.

Minik followed him trustingly.
After a while he said, "I like being
with you. You protect me. Will you
be my big brother?"
Big Bear laughed. "How can I be your
big brother? We're much too different!"

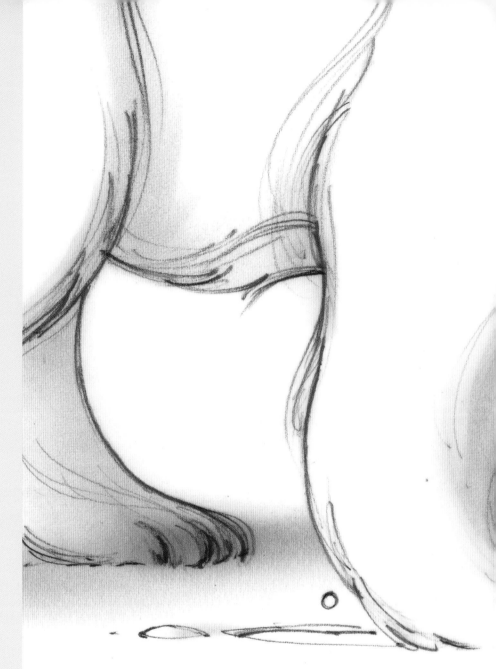

Minik led Big Bear to the edge of the water, and
they leant down to stare at themselves. "Look!" said Minik.
"We're not that different. We look just like each other when we smile!"

"Well, maybe," said Big Bear, "but I'm much taller than you."
Minik climbed onto a mound of snow.
"Not any more, you're not!" he laughed.
"Now I'm taller than you!"

"But I can be terrifying!" said Big Bear.
To prove it, he growled loudly.
Minik climbed down, pretended he was a fearsome pirate, and shouted in his loudest voice, "I'M NOT SCARED OF YOU!"

Big Bear laughed. "But I'm much faster than you!" he said. He started to run, and then slid onto his back. Minik jumped on, and together they skidded quickly over the ice.

"Look, I'm as fast as you!" Minik cried.

"Now watch me do some things I'm really good at!" said Minik.

He danced,

juggled a snowball,

and walked on his hands.
Big Bear tried to copy him.

"You're right that we're different," laughed Minik.
"But we don't have to be the same to be brothers, do we?"

Big Bear didn't reply. He had sensed
a storm suddenly approaching.

"We must go!" he said. "Walk close to
me, as quickly as you can. My body
will protect you from the wind."

The wind raged and heavy snow fell.
"Don't be afraid!" Big Bear shouted.
"I'll take you home, Little Brother!"

As the storm grew more violent, Minik became
exhausted. Twice he stumbled and almost fell.
Eventually he stopped – he could go no further.

Big Bear growled against the storm, but the wind drowned him out.
Minik began to grow faint, so Big Bear pulled him in close,
desperately trying to warm him.

Just then a bright light shone in front of them. Headlights!
A man appeared on a sled. Big Bear stopped dead.
This must be a hunter, and he was angry!
But Minik threw himself in front of Big Bear.

"Now it's my turn to protect you,
Big Brother," he said.

Then suddenly Minik ran towards the hunter.
"It's Daddy!" he shouted. "Daddy, stop! It's okay.
Big Bear is my brother. He saved my life!"

"Minik, my little boy!" cried his father.
"I've looked everywhere for you.
Are you all right?"

Minik didn't reply. He had seen
Big Bear turning to leave.
"Wait, Big Brother!" he cried.

He ran to him and held him tight.
"Goodbye, Big Brother!" he said.
"I'll never forget you."
"And you'll live in my heart forever,
Little Brother," said Big Bear.

Minik left on his father's sled, turning to watch
Big Bear as he disappeared into the distance.
The storm had died down as quickly as it had come.

Minik listened to the wind, now blowing gently.
How wonderful it was to be still . . .
to close his eyes . . . to dream!

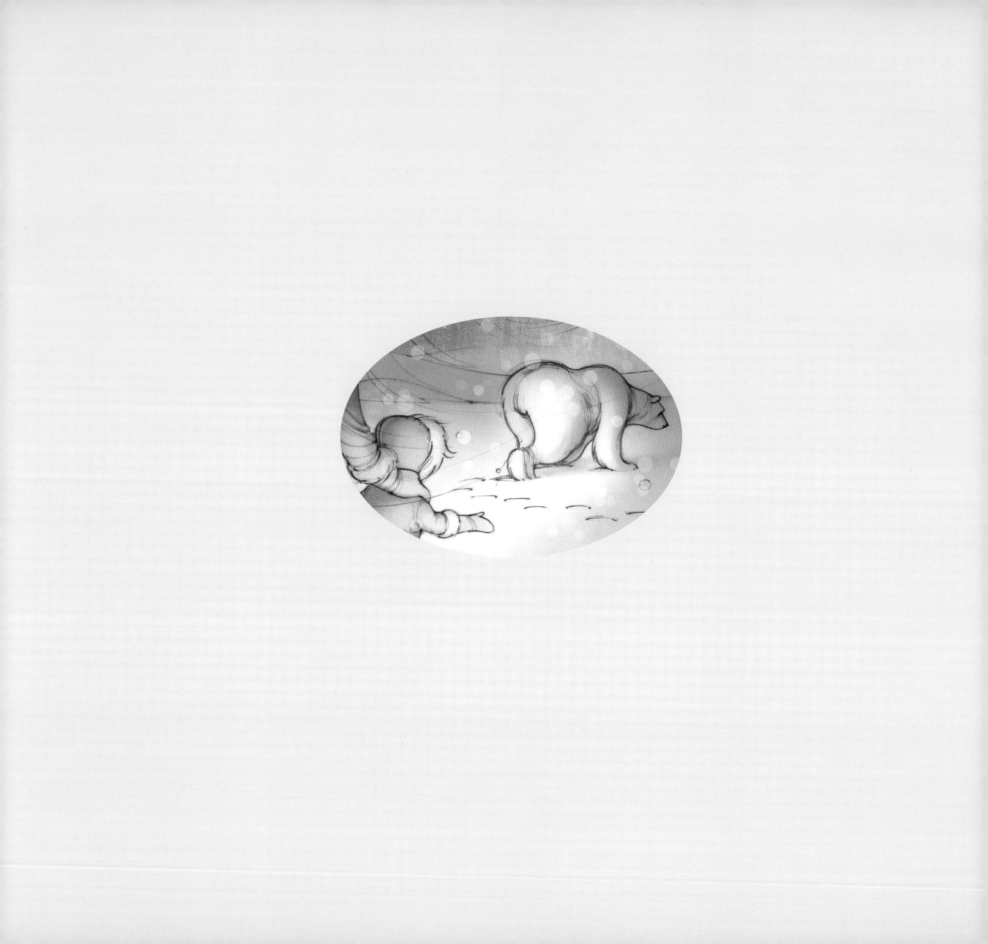